Lilla's Sunflowers

Written and Illustrated
by Colleen Rowan Kosinski

SKY PONY PRESS
NEW YORK

To Madison,
Spread the sunshine!
Colleen Rowan Kosinski

Cicadas sang their summer song.
The scent of green grass tickled Lilla's nose.
Lilla smiled.

Surrounded by sunflowers, Lilla and Papa tilted their faces toward the sun and basked in its warmth.

Before Papa left for a long trip far away,
Lilla gave him a sunflower seed.

"To remember me," Lilla whispered.

Papa was gone all fall, winter, and into spring.
Lilla covered her sunflower seeds with warm soil
and thought of Papa.

A breeze lifted Lilla's hair. It reminded her of Papa's last kiss.

Soon, seedlings appeared. "Hello there."

Lilla's sunflowers grew taller and stronger.

On long summer nights while fireflies flitted in the twilight, Lilla told her sunflowers stories about Papa.

Summer slipped away, and Papa had not returned.
The sunflowers' stalks became brittle and brown.

Every day they drooped a bit more.
So did Lilla.

One morning, Lilla found birds pecking at her precious sunflowers' faces.

"Mama, now Papa will never see my sunflowers," Lilla cried.

"There will be more summers filled with sunflowers to show Papa," Mama whispered.

Lilla didn't want to think about next summer.
It was too far away. She trudged inside.

A letter addressed to Lilla lay on the kitchen table. She carefully opened it.

Dear Darling Lilla,

I'm coming home! See you soon, my little sunflower!

Love,
Papa

P.S. I planted your seed. Look what happened!

Lilla danced outside. "Papa's coming home! And he did see one of my flowers this year."

Winter came and went. The next spring, Lilla and
Papa planted more of Lilla's sunflower seeds.
By summer the blooms were as big as dinner plates.

Soon letters began arriving from all over the country!

Papa explained, "Your sunflower was a bright spot for everyone while I was away. Before I left I gave a seed to each of my pals to plant in their own garden. Your sunflowers will bloom all across the country."

Lilla lay in the cool grass. From one seed
many flowers grew and made people happy.
Cicadas sang their summer song.
The scent of green grass tickled Lilla's nose.
And Lilla smiled.

I'd like to dedicate this book to all my writing friends, especially my picture book critiquers—Tanja Bauerle, Kristen Abbot, Jason Kirschner, Suzi Ryan, Tanya Anderson, and especially Dawn Young, who read countless versions. A big thanks to my fantastic agent, Isabel Atherton, my wonderful editor, Julie Matysik, and my wise friend, Steve Meltzer.

A special thank you to my husband, Chip, and my children, Colin, Taylor, and Alek, who always believed in me.

Thank you to all the men and women who serve our country to protect our freedom.

Sky Pony Press books may be purchased in bulk at special discounts for sales promotion, corporate gifts, fund-raising, or educational purposes. Special editions can also be created to specifications. For details, contact the Special Sales Department, Sky Pony Press, 307 West 36th Street, 11th Floor, New York, NY 10018 or info@skyhorsepublishing.com.

Sky Pony® is a registered trademark of Skyhorse Publishing, Inc.®, a Delaware corporation.

Visit our website at www.skyponypress.com.

10 9 8 7 6 5 4 3 2 1

Manufactured in China, March 2016
This product conforms to CPSIA 2008

Library of Congress Cataloging-in-Publication Data is available on file.

Cover design by Sarah Brody
Cover illustration credit Colleen Rowan Kosinski

Print ISBN: 978-1-5107-0464-0
Ebook ISBN: 978-1-5107-0468-8